U.S.A. TRAVEL GUIDES

PUERTO RICO

BY ANN HEINRICHS • ILLUSTRATED BY MATT KANIA

The Child's World®

childsworld.com

Published by The Child's World®
1980 Lookout Drive • Mankato, MN 56003-1705
800-599-READ • www.childsworld.com

Photo Credits

Photographs ©: iStockphoto, cover, 1, 15, 16, 20, 35, 38
(left); Felix Lipov/Shutterstock Images, 7; W. Marissen/
iStockphoto, 8; Herminio Rodriguez/AP Images, 11; John
& Lisa Merrill/DanitaDelimont.com "Danita Delimont
Photography"/Newscom, 12; Justin Smith/Shutterstock
Images, 19; Glynnis Jones/Shutterstock Images, 23;
Historic American Buildings Survey/Historic American
Engineering Record/Historic American Landscapes
Survey/Library of Congress, 24; Greg O'Bagel/
iStockphoto, 27; Isaac Ruiz/iStockphoto, 28; Herminio J.
Rodriguez/AP Images, 31; John Kershner/Shutterstock
Images, 32; Shutterstock Images, 38 (right)

ISBN 9781503819924
LCCN 2016961193

Printing

Printed in the United States of America
PA02334

About the Author
Ann Heinrichs

Ann Heinrichs is the author of more than 100 books for children and young adults. She has also enjoyed successful careers as a children's book editor and an advertising copywriter. Ann grew up in Fort Smith, Arkansas, and lives in Chicago, Illinois.

post card

About the
Map Illustrator
Matt Kania

Matt Kania loves maps and, as a kid, dreamed of making them. In school he studied geography and cartography, and today he makes maps for a living. Matt's favorite thing about drawing maps is learning about the places they represent. Many of the maps he has created can be found in books, magazines, videos, Web sites, and public places.

post card

*On the cover: Admire stunning sunsets from
Castillo San Felipe del Morro Fortress.*

OUR PUERTO RICO TRIP

Puerto Rico 4

Exploring Río Camuy Cave Park 7

Wildlife in El Yunque Rain Forest 8

Get Glowing in Mosquito Bay! 11

Tibes Indian Ceremonial Center 12

Ponce de León and Caparra 15

Strolling through Old San Juan 16

Hacienda Buena Vista Plantation 19

Maricao's Coffee Harvest Festival 20

Loíza's Saint James Festival 23

Sugar Mills, Old and New 24

La Fortaleza 27

Arecibo Observatory 28

The Three Kings of Juana Díaz 31

Saints at the Gate of Heaven 32

Maunabo's Lighthouse 35

Our Trip 36

Official Song 37

Official Symbols 37

Famous People 38

Words to Know 38

Official Flag and Seal 38

To Learn More 39

Index 40

PUERTO RICO

Are you ready to explore Puerto Rico? Just look what's in store for you!

You'll visit **plantations** and forts. You'll see where Puerto Rico's early peoples played ball. You'll enjoy lots of colorful festivals. You'll swim among tiny sea creatures that glow. You'll hike through a **rain forest**. And you'll explore some spooky caves!

There's much more to discover, so buckle up. We're off to Puerto Rico!

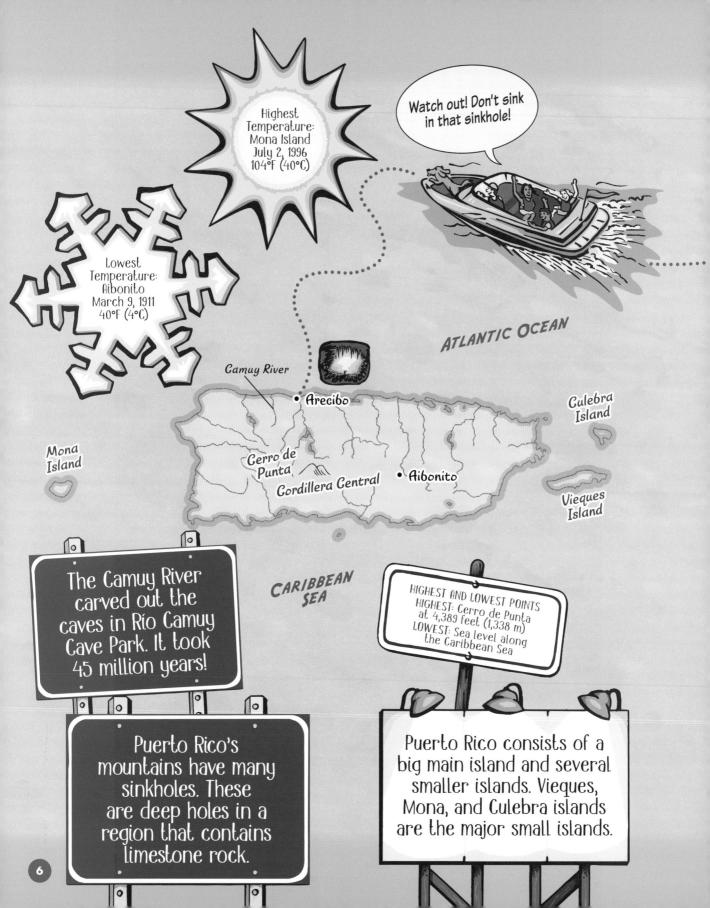

Highest Temperature: Mona Island July 2, 1996 104°F (40°C)

Watch out! Don't sink in that sinkhole!

Lowest Temperature: Aibonito March 9, 1911 40°F (4°C)

ATLANTIC OCEAN

Camuy River

• Arecibo

Culebra Island

Mona Island

Cerro de Punta

Cordillera Central

• Aibonito

Vieques Island

CARIBBEAN SEA

The Camuy River carved out the caves in Río Camuy Cave Park. It took 45 million years!

HIGHEST AND LOWEST POINTS
HIGHEST: Cerro de Punta at 4,389 feet (1,338 m)
LOWEST: Sea level along the Caribbean Sea

Puerto Rico's mountains have many sinkholes. These are deep holes in a region that contains limestone rock.

Puerto Rico consists of a big main island and several smaller islands. Vieques, Mona, and Culebra islands are the major small islands.

EXPLORING RÍO CAMUY CAVE PARK

You wander down the leafy green path. At last, you enter a spectacular cave. Its sparkling rock formations take your breath away!

You're exploring Río Camuy Cave Park. It's in the hills southwest of Arecibo.

Puerto Rico lies southeast of Florida. To the north is the Atlantic Ocean. To the south is the Caribbean Sea.

Puerto Rico's biggest cities are near the coast. Miles of sandy beaches line the coasts. Palm trees wave in the warm breezes there. Away from the coast, the land becomes hilly. Rugged mountains run across central Puerto Rico. The highest mountain range is the Cordillera Central.

Discover neat rock formations at Río Camuy Cave Park.

WILDLIFE IN EL YUNQUE RAIN FOREST

You brush past giant tree ferns. High overhead, leafy treetops block the sunlight. Thick vines hang down from the branches. A bright green parrot flits by. Suddenly, you hear a chirpy song. It's not a bird. It's a tiny tree frog, the coquí!

You're hiking through El Yunque National Forest. It's in the mountains west of Fajardo.

Puerto Rico is home to many other animals. The long, slender mongoose feasts on snakes. Lots of bats live in the island's caves. Wild goats live on Mona Island. Giant iguanas live there, too!

Many birds live in El Yunque National Forest, including the Puerto Rican tody.

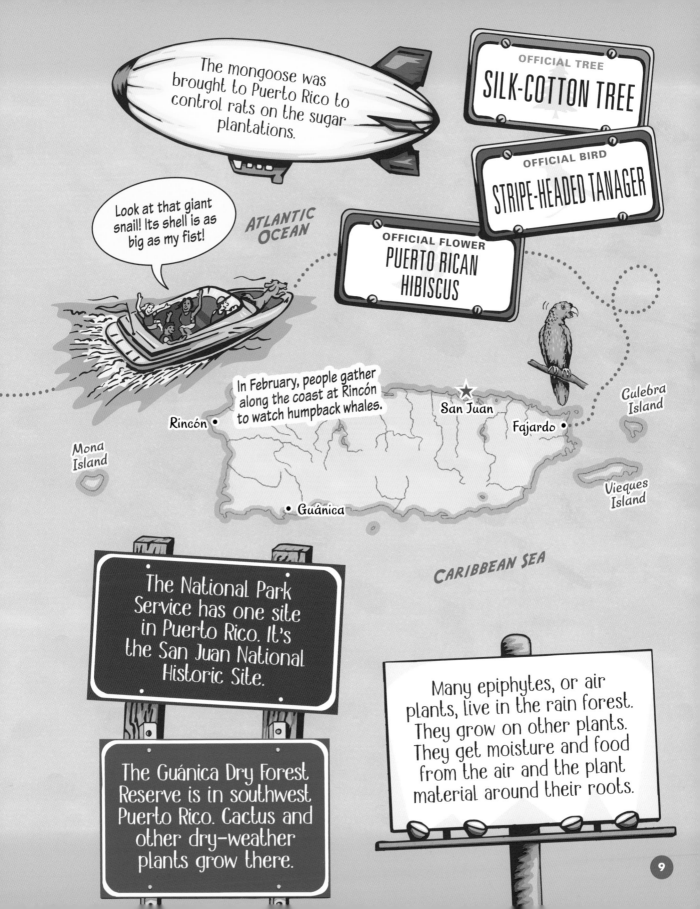

The mongoose was brought to Puerto Rico to control rats on the sugar plantations.

OFFICIAL TREE
SILK-COTTON TREE

OFFICIAL BIRD
STRIPE-HEADED TANAGER

OFFICIAL FLOWER
PUERTO RICAN HIBISCUS

Look at that giant snail! Its shell is as big as my fist!

ATLANTIC OCEAN

In February, people gather along the coast at Rincón to watch humpback whales.

Rincón •

★ San Juan

Fajardo •

Culebra Island

Mona Island

Vieques Island

• Guánica

CARIBBEAN SEA

The National Park Service has one site in Puerto Rico. It's the San Juan National Historic Site.

The Guánica Dry Forest Reserve is in southwest Puerto Rico. Cactus and other dry-weather plants grow there.

Many epiphytes, or air plants, live in the rain forest. They grow on other plants. They get moisture and food from the air and the plant material around their roots.

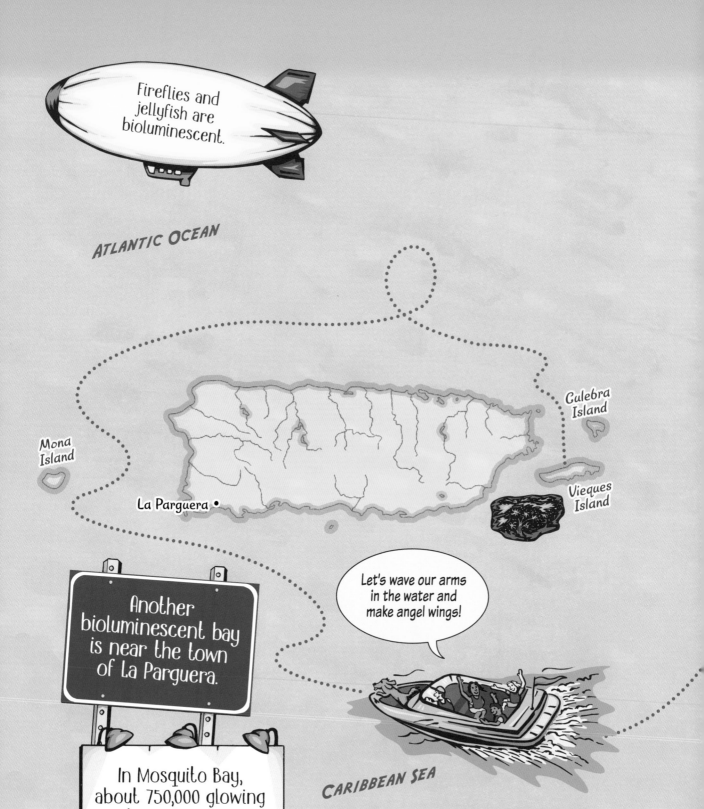

GET GLOWING IN MOSQUITO BAY!

Your boat glides along in the night. The water shimmers with a blue-green glow. Swish your fingers around in the water. It lights up like sparkling glitter!

You're cruising through Vieques Island's Mosquito Bay. Billions of tiny sea creatures live there. They light up when they're disturbed. Just try jumping in the water. You'll be dripping with sparkly water drops!

Mosquito Bay is also called Bioluminescent Bay. A bioluminescent creature is one that produces light. When's the best time to visit Mosquito Bay? On a cloudless night when the moon's not out!

Puerto Rico has a total of three bioluminescent bays that visitors can enjoy.

TIBES INDIAN CEREMONIAL CENTER

How did Puerto Rico's early people live? Just visit Tibes Indian Ceremonial Center near Ponce. It features a rebuilt Taíno village. The Taíno people occupied Tibes more than 1,000 years ago. They called their homeland Boriquén, or Borinquen.

You'll see Taíno *bohios*, or thatched-roof huts. You'll also see *bateyes*, or ball courts. People played a game like soccer there. Stones outline the borders of the courts. Some stones have petroglyphs, or carved pictures.

Christopher Columbus sailed to Puerto Rico in 1493. He claimed this land for Spain. He named it San Juan Bautista. That's Spanish for "Saint John the Baptist."

Check out the ball court at the Tibes Indian Ceremonial Center.

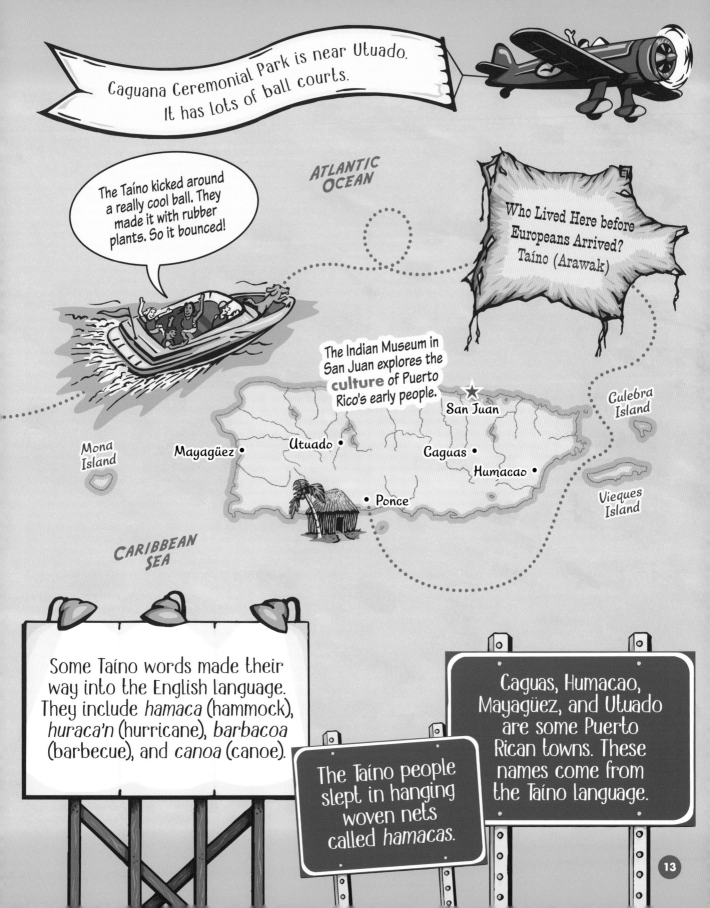

Caguana Ceremonial Park is near Utuado. It has lots of ball courts.

The Taíno kicked around a really cool ball. They made it with rubber plants. So it bounced!

ATLANTIC OCEAN

Who Lived Here before Europeans Arrived? Taíno (Arawak)

The Indian Museum in San Juan explores the **culture** of Puerto Rico's early people.

★ San Juan

Culebra Island

Mona Island

Mayagüez •

Utuado •

Caguas •

Humacao •

Vieques Island

CARIBBEAN SEA

• Ponce

Some Taíno words made their way into the English language. They include *hamaca* (hammock), *huraca'n* (hurricane), *barbacoa* (barbecue), and *canoa* (canoe).

The Taíno people slept in hanging woven nets called *hamacas*.

Caguas, Humacao, Mayagüez, and Utuado are some Puerto Rican towns. These names come from the Taíno language.

Puerto Rico was a Spanish **colony** from 1493 to 1898.

ATLANTIC OCEAN

Caparra •

Culebra Island

Mona Island

Vieques Island

CARIBBEAN SEA

At least some walls are still standing. Will our house look this good in 500 years?

The Caparra Ruins Historical Museum and Park contains the ruins of Ponce de León's house. Nearby is the Museum of the Conquest and Colonization of Puerto Rico.

PONCE DE LEÓN AND CAPARRA

Stroll around Caparra. It doesn't look like much today. But it was Puerto Rico's first Spanish settlement. Juan Ponce de León arrived there in 1508. He met the Taíno chief Agueybana.

Ponce de León established a plantation at Caparra. He became Puerto Rico's first Spanish governor. Later, more Spanish **colonists** arrived. They set up farms, forts, and towns. Some hunted for gold, too.

The Spaniards forced the Taíno people to work as slaves. Many Taínos were killed. Even more died of diseases brought by the Spaniards. Then African people were also brought in as slaves. They were forced to work in mines and on plantations.

This memorial for Ponce de León was built in 1540.

STROLLING THROUGH OLD SAN JUAN

The massive fort looks out over the sea. It's called El Morro. Spaniards built it to guard San Juan from attacks by sea. The fort's cannons could destroy enemy ships.

San Juan became the capital city in 1521. Now you can stroll through the city's old section. There you'll see many buildings from colonial times.

El Morro was not the city's only fort. San Cristóbal and El Cañuelo are two others. San Juan Cathedral stands in the old city, too. The body of Ponce de León rests there.

San Juan de la Cruz is the full name of the El Cañuelo fort.

Explore the colorful streets of Old San Juan.

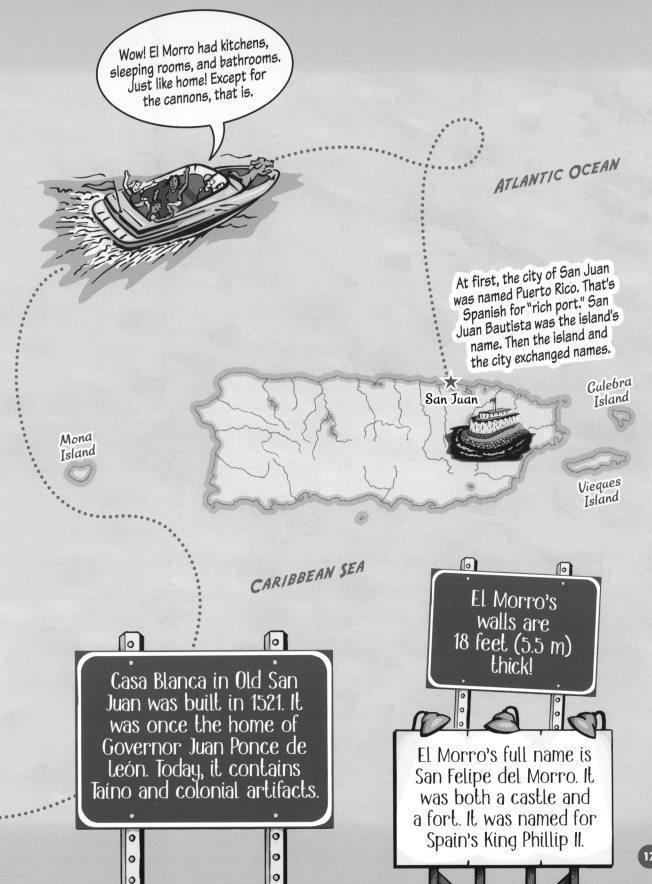

Wow! El Morro had kitchens, sleeping rooms, and bathrooms. Just like home! Except for the cannons, that is.

ATLANTIC OCEAN

At first, the city of San Juan was named Puerto Rico. That's Spanish for "rich port." San Juan Bautista was the island's name. Then the island and the city exchanged names.

San Juan

Culebra Island

Mona Island

Vieques Island

CARIBBEAN SEA

Casa Blanca in Old San Juan was built in 1521. It was once the home of Governor Juan Ponce de León. Today, it contains Taíno and colonial artifacts.

El Morro's walls are 18 feet (5.5 m) thick!

El Morro's full name is San Felipe del Morro. It was both a castle and a fort. It was named for Spain's King Phillip II.

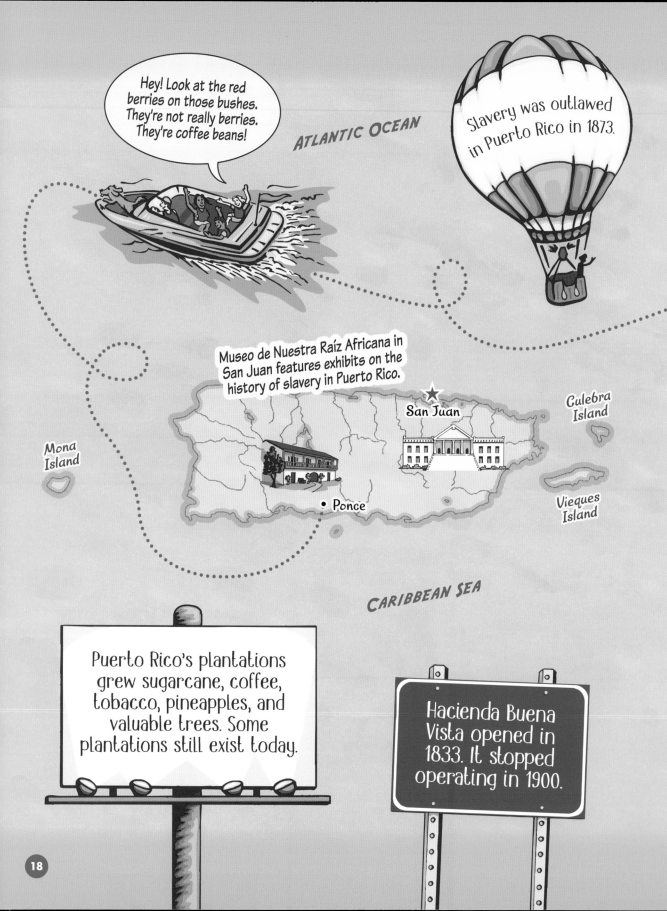

Farm animals roam around the grounds. There are slaves' quarters and horse stalls. Inside the mill, big machines are clanking. Take a trail through the forest. A sparkling waterfall rushes down the rocks. The water power runs the mill's machines.

You're touring Hacienda Buena Vista plantation. It's in the hills north of Ponce. Hacienda Buena Vista was a coffee plantation. The mill processed the coffee beans. It also ground corn into cornmeal.

Sugarcane was also an important crop by the 1800s. Thousands of enslaved people were forced to work on Puerto Rico's sugar plantations.

A sugar plantation house in Puerto Rico

MARICAO'S COFFEE HARVEST FESTIVAL

Folk dancers whirl around in their colorful costumes. Food stalls sell delicious coffee desserts. Everywhere, the smell of coffee fills the air. It's the Coffee Harvest Festival!

Coffee was introduced to Puerto Rico in the 1700s. Today, it's one of Puerto Rico's major crops. Much of it grows in the western highlands.

Plantains are one of Puerto Rico's leading fruits. They're a type of banana. Bananas, pineapples, mangoes, and avocados are also important. Sugarcane is a valuable crop, too. Many farmers raise milk cows and beef cattle.

Coffee beans are the seeds of coffee cherries.

San Juan hosts Saborea Puerto Rico. Visitors can taste samples from some of Puerto Rico's famous chefs and restaurants.

Yum! Try this coffee cake. They've got coffee candy, too!

ATLANTIC OCEAN

What Are Puerto Rico's Fishing Products? Lobsters and tuna

Mona Island

San Juan

Maricao

Aibonito

Culebra Island

Vieques Island

CARIBBEAN SEA

Aibonito holds a flower festival every year.

What Does Puerto Rico Raise? Milk, poultry products, coffee, and fruit

Puerto Rico's coffee comes from the Arabica coffee plant. This bushy plant produces bright red coffee beans.

In 2016, 3,411,307 people lived in Puerto Rico. In population, it ranks between 30th-ranked Iowa and 29th-ranked Connecticut.

Many of Loíza's early residents were Yoruba people from West Africa.

ATLANTIC OCEAN

San Juan
Bayamón
Carolina
Loíza

Culebra Island

Mona Island

Vieques Island

CARIBBEAN SEA

Puerto Rico's official languages are Spanish and English. But Spanish is the most widely spoken language.

Masks for the Saint James Festival are called *vejigante* masks. Traditionally, they're made with coconut shells and carved wood.

POPULATION OF LARGEST CITIES
San Juan.....................355,074
Bayamón.....................189,159
Carolina......................161,884

LOÍZA'S SAINT JAMES FESTIVAL

People are wearing baggy costumes. And their masks are a fright! They look like ugly monsters. Big fangs poke out of their fiery mouths. And long horns stick out from their heads!

You're watching the Saint James Festival in Loíza. It blends African and Spanish cultures. Many enslaved Africans once lived in Loíza. Most of the city's residents today have African roots. The masks grew out of African **traditions**.

Religious festivals are common in Puerto Rico. Each town has a **patron saint**. The saint's feast day is a big event. Processions move through the plaza, or town square. Then everyone enjoys music, dancing, and food.

Puerto Ricans also wear masks for Carnival, a celebration before the Christian season of Lent.

SUGAR MILLS, OLD AND NEW

Drive across the countryside in Puerto Rico. Here and there, you see tall brick chimneys. They are the ruins of old sugar mills. Blazing furnaces provided heat to process the sugarcane. The chimneys belched out smoke from the fires.

You can see Guánica's old sugar mill. It belonged to Hacienda Igualdad plantation. Manatí has an old mill, too. So do San Sebastián, Toa Baja, and Barceloneta.

Foods are valuable factory products in Puerto Rico. And sugar has been important for centuries. Sugar mills still turn sugarcane into sugar. Other factories make medicines, electrical equipment, and machines.

The Hacienda Azucarera la Igualdad plantation used a steam engine.

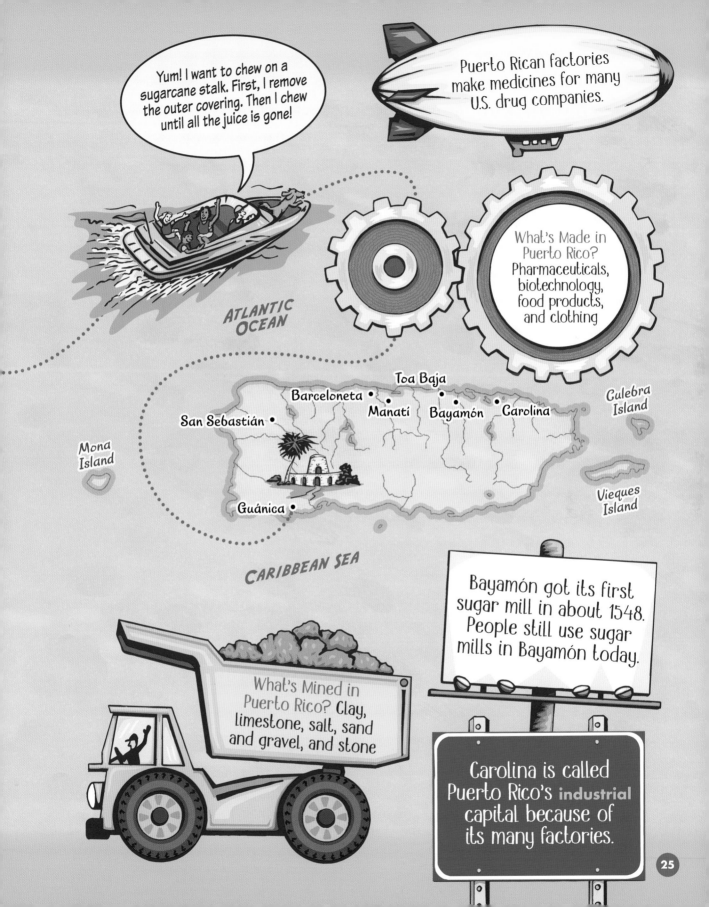

Yum! I want to chew on a sugarcane stalk. First, I remove the outer covering. Then I chew until all the juice is gone!

Puerto Rican factories make medicines for many U.S. drug companies.

What's Made in Puerto Rico? Pharmaceuticals, biotechnology, food products, and clothing

ATLANTIC OCEAN

Toa Baja

Barceloneta
Manatí   Bayamón   Carolina

San Sebastián

Culebra Island

Mona Island

Vieques Island

Guánica

CARIBBEAN SEA

Bayamón got its first sugar mill in about 1548. People still use sugar mills in Bayamón today.

What's Mined in Puerto Rico? Clay, limestone, salt, sand and gravel, and stone

Carolina is called Puerto Rico's industrial capital because of its many factories.

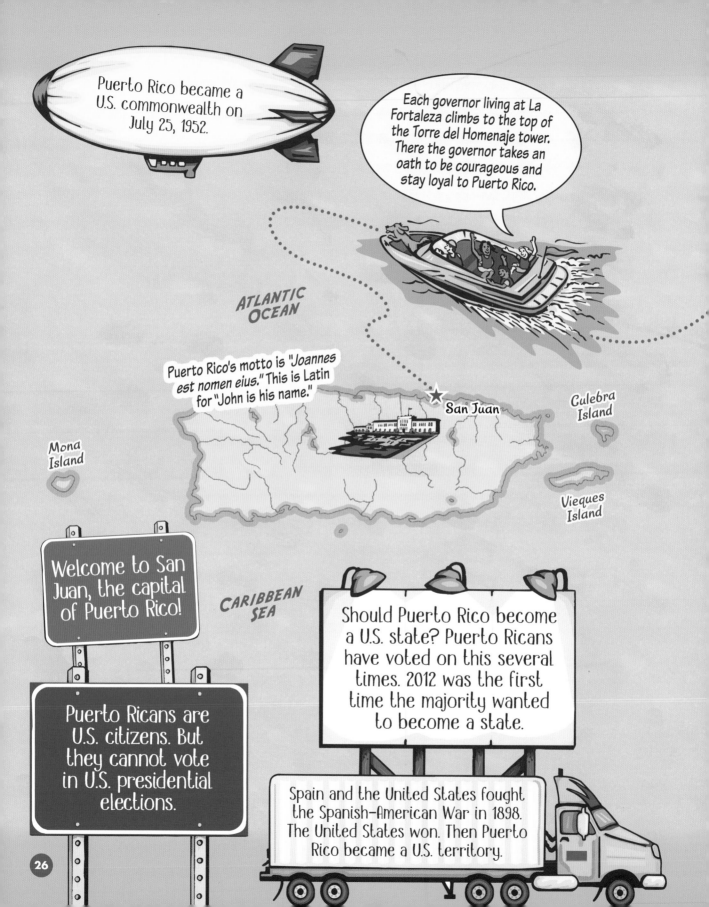

Puerto Rico became a U.S. commonwealth on July 25, 1952.

Each governor living at La Fortaleza climbs to the top of the Torre del Homenaje tower. There the governor takes an oath to be courageous and stay loyal to Puerto Rico.

ATLANTIC OCEAN

Puerto Rico's motto is "Joannes est nomen eius." This is Latin for "John is his name."

San Juan

Culebra Island

Mona Island

Vieques Island

Welcome to San Juan, the capital of Puerto Rico!

CARIBBEAN SEA

Should Puerto Rico become a U.S. state? Puerto Ricans have voted on this several times. 2012 was the first time the majority wanted to become a state.

Puerto Ricans are U.S. citizens. But they cannot vote in U.S. presidential elections.

Spain and the United States fought the Spanish-American War in 1898. The United States won. Then Puerto Rico became a U.S. territory.

La Fortaleza stands in Old San Juan. But is it a fort or a home? It's both. It was built as a fort in the 1500s. But it soon became the governor's **mansion**. Puerto Rico's governors still live and work there.

The United States took control of Puerto Rico in 1898. In 1952, it became a U.S. **commonwealth**. It formed a government with three branches. One branch makes laws. Its members meet in San Juan's capitol. Another branch carries out the laws. The governor heads this branch. Judges make up the third branch. They decide whether someone has broken the law.

The governor's mansion is inside the walls of La Fortaleza.

ARECIBO OBSERVATORY

Stand high on the platform. Look down at the big, curved dish. It could hold 26 football fields!

You're visiting Arecibo Observatory. It's up in the mountains south of Arecibo. It has a massive radio telescope.

The dish collects radio waves from space. Scientists study those waves. They learn about stars, planets, and other objects. Arecibo's scientists also work on the SETI project. SETI stands for "Search for **Extra-Terrestrial** Intelligence"!

U.S. organizations have many projects in Puerto Rico. Arecibo Observatory is one of them.

The Arecibo Observatory's dish is made of nearly 40,000 aluminum panels.

New York's Cornell University operates Arecibo Observatory.

ATLANTIC OCEAN

Mona Island

Arecibo

The observatory's dish lies inside a vast sinkhole.

Culebra Island

Vieques Island

Is anyone else out there? Let's see if they've picked up any messages from space!

CARIBBEAN SEA

The U.S. Navy used to test bombs on Vieques Island. Residents protested after an accidental death in 1999. The navy left Vieques in 2003.

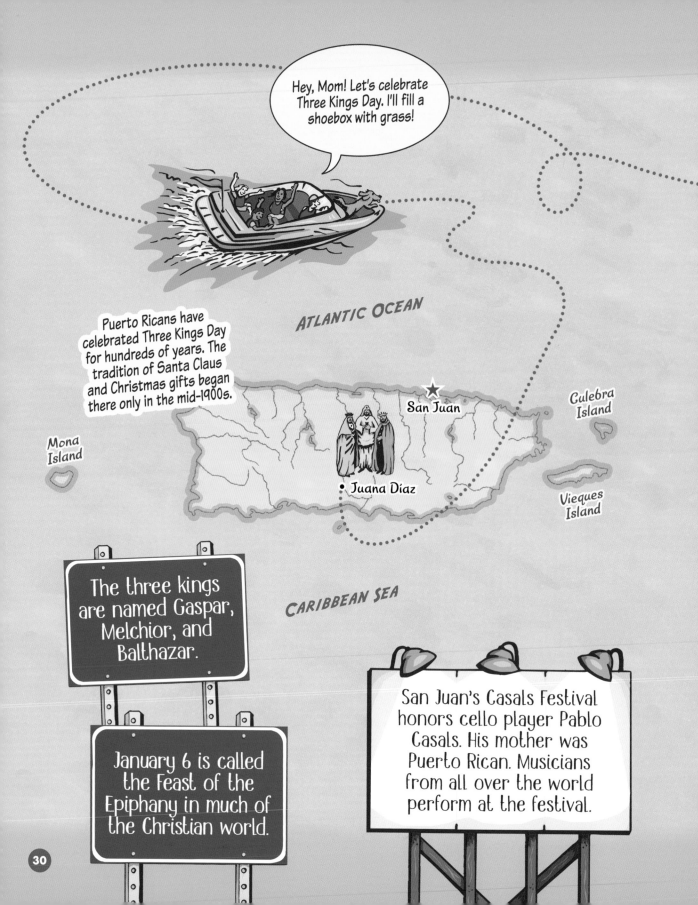

Hey, Mom! Let's celebrate Three Kings Day. I'll fill a shoebox with grass!

ATLANTIC OCEAN

Puerto Ricans have celebrated Three Kings Day for hundreds of years. The tradition of Santa Claus and Christmas gifts began there only in the mid-1900s.

★ San Juan

Culebra Island

Mona Island

• Juana Díaz

Vieques Island

CARIBBEAN SEA

The three kings are named Gaspar, Melchior, and Balthazar.

January 6 is called the Feast of the Epiphany in much of the Christian world.

San Juan's Casals Festival honors cello player Pablo Casals. His mother was Puerto Rican. Musicians from all over the world perform at the festival.

THE THREE KINGS OF JUANA DÍAZ

Children are excited. Tomorrow is Three Kings Day—January 6. The Three Kings will come in the night.

The children fill a shoebox with grass. They slip the box under their beds. It's for the kings' hungry camels or horses. In the morning, the grass is gone. The box is full of gifts!

Three Kings Day honors the three wise men. In Christian tradition, they visited the infant Jesus. In Juana Díaz, three men dress as the kings. They wear crowns and glittering robes. Children write them letters, telling the kings what gifts they want!

The Three Kings wait to meet with children.

Wander through the streets of San Germán. Climb the church steps to Porta Coeli. That means "Gate of Heaven"!

This old church was built in 1606. It's now a museum of religious art. There you'll see a display of *santos*. These are saints and other religious figures. Each one is hand carved from wood.

Carving *santos* is a fine Puerto Rican craft. Artists who carve them are called *santeros*. Many craftspeople also carve roosters and other birds. Some people weave hammocks. The Taíno people began this tradition.

The monastery, a place that houses monks, next to Porta Coeli is now in ruins.

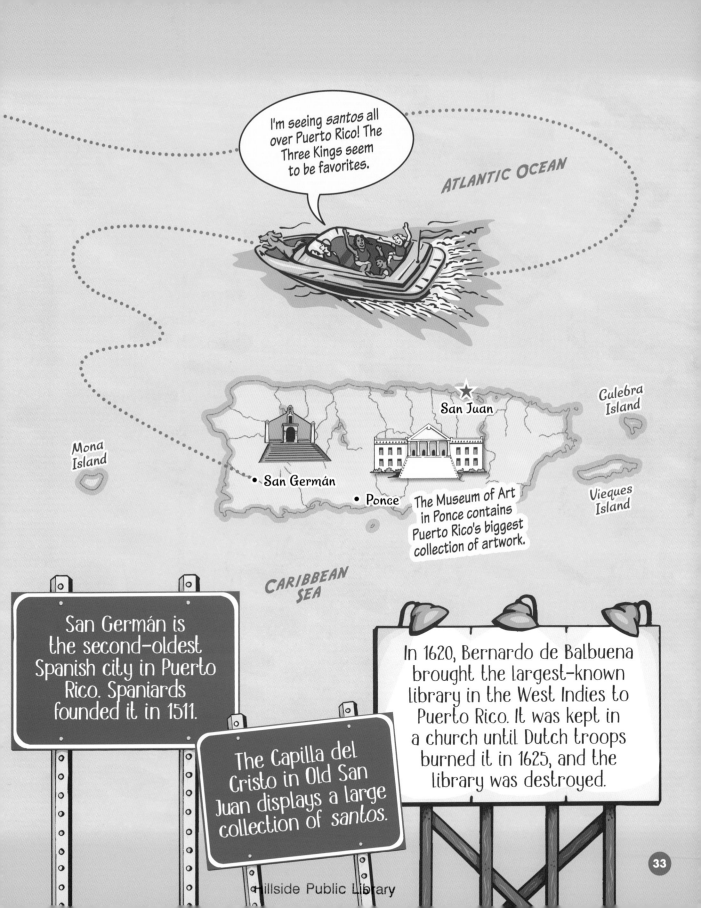

I'm seeing santos all over Puerto Rico! The Three Kings seem to be favorites.

ATLANTIC OCEAN

Mona Island

San Germán

Ponce

★ San Juan

The Museum of Art in Ponce contains Puerto Rico's biggest collection of artwork.

Culebra Island

Vieques Island

CARIBBEAN SEA

San Germán is the second-oldest Spanish city in Puerto Rico. Spaniards founded it in 1511.

The Capilla del Cristo in Old San Juan displays a large collection of santos.

In 1620, Bernardo de Balbuena brought the largest-known library in the West Indies to Puerto Rico. It was kept in a church until Dutch troops burned it in 1625, and the library was destroyed.

33

Hillside Public Library

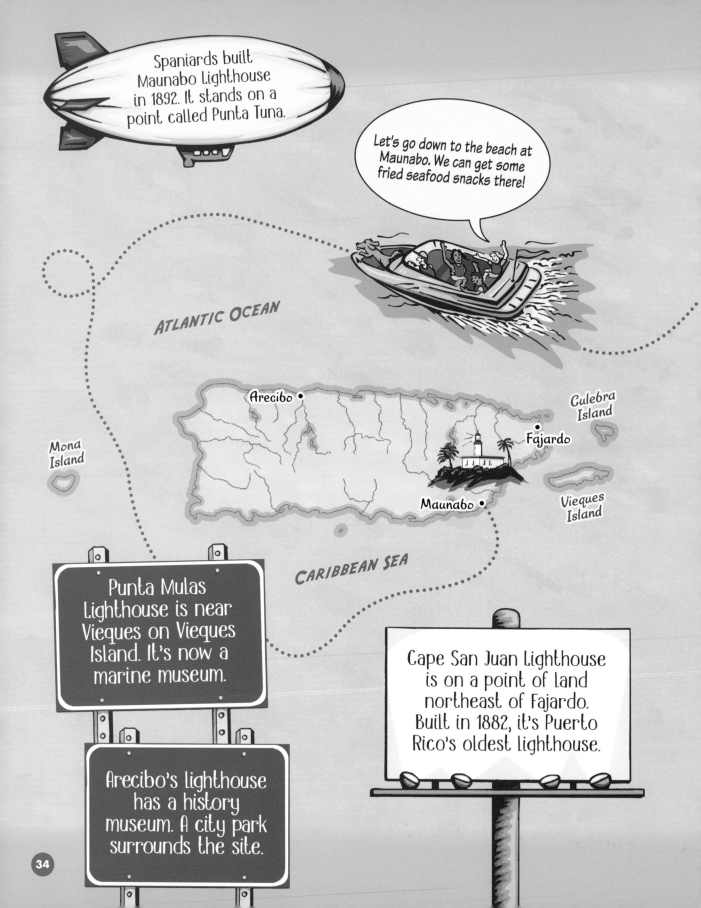

Spaniards built Maunabo Lighthouse in 1892. It stands on a point called Punta Tuna.

Let's go down to the beach at Maunabo. We can get some fried seafood snacks there!

ATLANTIC OCEAN

Arecibo •

Culebra Island

Mona Island

Fajardo •

Maunabo •

Vieques Island

CARIBBEAN SEA

Punta Mulas Lighthouse is near Vieques on Vieques Island. It's now a marine museum.

Cape San Juan Lighthouse is on a point of land northeast of Fajardo. Built in 1882, it's Puerto Rico's oldest lighthouse.

Arecibo's lighthouse has a history museum. A city park surrounds the site.

MAUNABO'S LIGHTHOUSE

Stroll down to the Punta Tuna lighthouse on the coast near Maunabo. You'll see why a lighthouse was built here. The waters are choppy along this rocky coast. The lighthouse blinks a bright signal. It warns ships to stay away from the shore.

Many other lighthouses stand along the coast. Some are still flashing their signals. And a few even have museums.

Spaniards built these lighthouses in the 1800s. Ship traffic was much heavier then. Why not visit a lighthouse? Just watch out for those crashing waves!

Stop at the beach while visiting the Punta Tuna lighthouse.

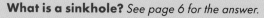

OUR TRIP

We visited many amazing places on our trip! We also met a lot of interesting people along the way. Look at the map below. Use your finger to trace all the places we have been.

What is a sinkhole? *See page 6 for the answer.*

What are Puerto Rico's major small islands? *See page 6 for the answer.*

Why was the mongoose brought to Puerto Rico? *See page 9 for the answer.*

What do fireflies and jellyfish have in common? *See page 10 for the answer.*

What Taíno words are used in the English language? *See page 13 for the answer.*

When was Puerto Rico a Spanish colony? *See page 14 for the answer.*

What are Puerto Rico's official languages? *See page 22 for the answer.*

What are the three kings' names? *See page 30 for the answer.*

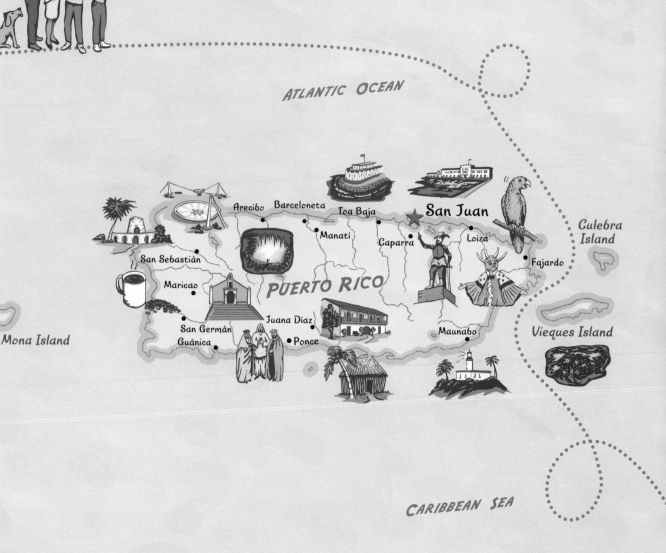

ATLANTIC OCEAN

Arecibo Barceloneta Toa Baja San Juan Culebra Island

Manati Caparra Loiza

San Sebastián Fajardo

Maricao PUERTO RICO

Juana Díaz Maunabo Vieques Island

San Germán Ponce

Guánica

Mona Island

CARIBBEAN SEA

OFFICIAL SONG

"LA BORINQUEÑA"

Original words and music by Felix Astol y Artés;
new words by Manuel Fernández Juncos;
new musical arrangement by Ramón Collado

Spanish:
La tierra de Borinquén
donde he nacido yo,
es un jardín florido
de mágico fulgor.

Un cielo siempre nítido
le sirve de dosel
y dan arrullos plácidos
las olas a sus pies.

Cuando a sus playas llegó Colón;
Exclamó lleno de admiración;
"Oh!, oh!, oh!, esta es la linda
tierra que busco yo."

Es Borinquen la hija,
la hija del mar y el sol,
del mar y el sol,
del mar y el sol,
del mar y el sol,
del mar y el sol.

English:
The land of Borinquen
where I have been born,
It is a florid garden
of magical brilliance.

A sky always clean
serves as a canopy,
And placid lullabies are given
by the waves at her feet.

When at her beaches Columbus
arrived,
he exclaimed full of admiration:
"Oh! Oh! Oh!
This is the beautiful land that I seek."

It is Borinquen the daughter,
the daughter of the sea and the sun,
of the sea and the sun,
of the sea and the sun,
of the sea and the sun,
of the sea and the sun!

That was a great trip! We have traveled all over Puerto Rico! There were a few places we didn't have time for, though. Next time, we plan to visit Culebra National Wildlife Refuge on Culebra Island. Two types of sea turtles make their nests on the refuge. Visitors can hike, bird-watch, and take pictures of the diverse nature.

OFFICIAL SYMBOLS

Official bird: Reina mora (stripe-headed tanager)
Official flower: Flor de maga (Puerto Rican hibiscus)
Official tree: Ceiba (silk-cotton tree)
Popular animal symbol: Coquí (tree frog)

FAMOUS PEOPLE

Albizu Campos, Pedro (1891–1965), political activist

Andino, Paola (1998–), actor

Anthony, Marc (1968–), singer, songwriter, and actor born to Puerto Rican parents

Baez, Javier (1992–), baseball player

Barbosa, José Celso (1857–1921), politician

Campeche, José (1751–1809), painter

Clemente, Roberto (1934–1972), baseball player

Del Toro, Benicio (1967–), actor

Garcia, Ricky (1999–), singer

Julia, Raul (1940–1994), actor

Lindor, Francisco (1993–), baseball player

Martin, Ricky (1971–), singer

Phoenix, Joaquin (1974–), actor

Ruiz Belvis, Segundo (1829–1867), abolitionist

Trinidad, Félix "Tito" (1973–), boxer

WORDS TO KNOW

colonists (KOL-uh-nists) people who settle a new land for their home country

colony (KOL-uh-nee) a land settled and governed by another country

commonwealth (KOM-uhn-welth) name for a state, country, or group of nations; also, a territory tied to the United States but having self-government

culture (KUL-chur) a people's beliefs, customs, and way of life

extra-terrestrial (X-truh tur-RES-tree-uhl) from outer space

industrial (in-DUH-stree-uhl) having to do with businesses and factories

mansion (MAN-shuhn) a large, elegant house

patron saint (PAY-truhn SAYNT) a saint who has a special meaning to a certain group of people

plantations (plan-TAY-shuhnz) large farms that usually raise one main crop

rain forest (RAYN FOR-uhst) a forest that gets very heavy rainfall and has tall, broad-leaved evergreen trees

traditions (truh-DISH-uhnz) long-held customs

-12

Official flag

Official seal

TO LEARN MORE

IN THE LIBRARY

Bjorklund, Ruth, and Richard Hantula. *Puerto Rico.* 3rd ed. New York, NY: Cavendish Square, 2016.

Roth, Susan L., and Cindy Trumbore. *Parrots over Puerto Rico.* New York, NY: Lee and Low Books, 2013.

ON THE WEB

Visit our Web site for links about Puerto Rico:

childsworld.com/links

Note to Parents, Teachers, and Librarians: We routinely verify our Web links to make sure they are safe and active sites. So encourage your readers to check them out!

PLACES TO VISIT OR CONTACT

Lonely Planet

lonelyplanet.com/puerto-rico
For more information about things to see and do in Puerto Rico.

Puerto Rico Tourism Company

seepuertorico.com
800/866-7827
For more information about traveling in Puerto Rico

Puerto Rico covers 5,325 square miles (13,791 sq km). In size, it's between 48th-ranked Connecticut and 49th-ranked Delaware.

INDEX

A

Agueybana, 15
Aibonito, 6, 21
animals, 8, 9, 19, 20
Arecibo, 7, 28, 34
Arecibo Observatory, 28, 29

B

Balbuena, Bernardo de, 33
Barceloneta, 24
Bayamón, 22, 25
bioluminescence, 10, 11

C

Caguas, 13
Camuy River, 6
Caparra Ruins Historical Museum and Park, 14
Cape San Juan Lighthouse, 34
Capilla del Cristo, 33
Carolina, 22, 25
Casa Blanca, 17
Casals, Pablo, 30
Casals Festival, 30
climate, 6
coffee, 18, 19, 20, 21
Coffee Harvest Festival, 20
colonists, 15
Columbus, Christopher, 12
commonwealth, 26, 27
Cordillera Central, 7
Cornell University, 29
Culebra Island, 6

E

El Cañuelo, 16
El Morro, 16, 17
El Yunque National Forest, 8
elevation, 6

F

Fajardo, 8, 34
Feast of the Epiphany, 30

G

Guánica, 9, 24
Guánica Dry Forest Reserve, 9

H

Hacienda Buena Vista, 18, 19
Hacienda Igualdad, 24
Humacao, 13

J

Juana Díaz, 31

K

King Phillip II, 17

L

La Fortaleza, 26, 27
La Parguera, 10
Loíza, 22, 23

M

Manatí, 24
Maunabo Lighthouse, 34, 35
Mayagüez, 13
mining, 15, 25
Mona Island, 6, 8
Mosquito Bay, 10, 11
Museo de Nuestra Raíz Africana, 18
Museum of Art, 33
Museum of the Conquest and Colonization of Puerto Rico, 14

O

official languages, 22
official symbols, 5, 9, 26

P

plantations, 9, 15, 18
plants, 9, 18, 19, 20, 21
Ponce, 12, 19, 33
Ponce de León, Juan, 14, 15, 16, 17
population, 22
Porta Coeli, 32
Punta Mulas Lighthouse, 34
Punta Tuna Lighthouse, 35

R

Río Camuy Cave Park, 6, 7

S

Saborea Puerto Rico, 21
Saint James Festival, 22, 23
San Cristóbal, 16
San Germán, 32, 33
San Juan, 13, 16, 17, 18, 21, 22, 27, 30, 33
San Juan Bautista, 12, 17
San Juan Cathedral, 16
San Juan National Historic Site, 9
San Sebastián, 24
santeros, 32
santos, 32, 33
SETI project, 28
sinkholes, 6, 29
slavery, 15, 18, 19, 23
Spanish-American War, 26
sugarcane, 18, 19, 20, 24, 25

T

Taíno, 12, 13, 15, 17, 32
Three Kings Day, 30, 31
Tibes Indian Ceremonial Center, 12
Toa Baja, 24

U

U.S. Navy, 29
Utuado, 13

V

vejigante masks, 22
Vieques, 34
Vieques Island, 6, 11, 29, 34

Bye, Island of Enchantment. We had a great time. We'll come back soon!